John J Culkin

Reuben Flood

Other titles by the Author

Pay the Devil
A Darkness in the light

A string of pearls
{With NAC writers}

Rotunda ramblings
Take me to another place.
{With Rotunda writers}

Scotty Road writers in Black and White
{With SRW}

Cover by John S Culkin
Reuben Flood

"My hero's have always been cowboys and they still are it seems."

From the album *"A Horse called Music."*

By Willie Nelson

If like me and all my school mates, you were born just after the Second World War in Liverpool, then the streets of houses that the Luftwaffe had reduced to rubble became your playground.

My mates and I would go to the Saturday morning Flicks to watch the western serials. Then on the sites of flattened houses we would re-enact whatever picture we had just watched at The Sun Hall Picture House, on Stanley Road in Bootle Merseyside

Saturdays were Hopalong Cassidy, Johnny Mcbrown, Lash La rue, Jack Elam and the wonderful Gabby Hayes.

As I grew older my heroes metamorphosed into Glenn Ford, Jack Palance, Clint Eastwood, Steve McQueen and Yul Brynner.

I hope that my tale of the American West does justice to all of the great cowboys that kept me entertained as a nine year old boy and who still do as the seventy three year old that I am today.

John J culkin

Special thanks

Firstly to my son, John Stephen Culkin, without his patience and knowledge of all thinks related to computers, this book might never have been printed.

Secondly, to all of my childhood friends who as nine and ten year old boys turned those bombed out streets of Liverpool's dockland into the Wild West.

And finally to June Davies my tutor at the Rotunda Creative Writing class. Many thank's June for constructive criticism and mega inspiration.

1

West Texas
Spring 1880

The city of Denver was six weeks behind him. Denver and the state of Colorado were probably still under a deep covering of snow. Now he was in the southern state of Texas, and whatever winter snow remained was only visible on the high peaks of the Guadalupe Mountains in the far west of that State.

The four hundred mile journey was hard on him, but it was harder on old Dan. Dan was the six year old strawberry roan that he had raised from a foal.

The horse was in need of a long rest and some good corn feed. It had existed on scrub grass for the last two weeks of the punishing journey. The five dollars he'd spent on having Dan re-shod in Santa Fe New Mexico had saved the horse from going lame. If that had happened then he would have had to shoot the animal. He pushed the dark thought to the back of his mind.

The solitary tree which he had passed on the outskirts of El Paso was just coming into leaf; if he could get his business done then he would be back in Colorado before the spring blossoms had fallen from its branches.

He led the horse to the town's Smithy which was housed in a wooden built forge on the only road that went in and out of El Paso. Reuben Flood asked the man to clean the horse up and feed him a corn ration. He inquired the cost to have Dan reshod for the second time on this trek. It had been a bone wearying journey that had taken him a month and a half and it would not end until he was back in Denver in the high summer. The horse had stood up well to the long trek, but he knew it would require a long rest and the best feed that money could buy if the animal was to complete the return journey.

'For a corn feed, shoes and stabling, ten dollars mister.' The big round shouldered blacksmith shaded his eyes from the morning sunshine. He waited patiently for the stranger to make up his mind.

Flood opened the saddle bags and took out a brown leather pouch. The blacksmith watched impassively as the stranger who was covered in a grey layer of trail dust fished out a ten dollar coin.

The pouch looked heavy; He'll need to be careful in this town, the blacksmith thought. Once the local card sharks got wind of the stranger with a pocket full of dollars, they'd fall on him like coyotes on a week old desert carcase.

Flood flipped the gold coin in the Smithy's direction and as big and awkward as he looked, the man moved swiftly to snatch the coin from the air before it reached the red dust that covered what passed for the main street.

'I'll be here for a week.' Flood used his Stetson to beat the weeks of trail dust from his pants and shirt. 'You look after old Dan here 'till then and there's another ten dollars in it for you.'

A huge grin stretched itself across the smithy's face. 'No problem friend, your horse will be ready when you want him.' He pointed to the north end of the dusty street. 'The saloon and the only hotel in town is that way mister.'

The blacksmith pointed in the direction of El Paso's only drinking establishment. 'I reckon the hotel first friend, cos you stink real bad mister an' I reckon a bath wouldn't go amiss.'

Flood treated the man to a sour grin and then made his way to Gannon's First Class Hotel.

He smiled and sighed contentedly as he slipped into the tin bath of hot water, counting himself lucky that he was the first user of that particular water on that day. 'I suppose it can call itself first class, if it's the only hotel for fifty miles,' Reuben thought as he relaxed for the first time in weeks. The reason for his journey was pushed to the back of a tired mind.

The Blacksmith was right though, he really needed this bath and his body had reeked with the odour of stale dried sweat. He always carried the stink of horse about his body, so Dan's smell didn't bother him, but even he had to admit that after all those weeks in the saddle he stank something awful.

The Smithy had wrinkled his nose as Flood had passed him Dan's reins, not everyone it seemed, was indifferent to his ripe odour.

*

He felt like a new man as he strode toward the saloon. The bath had removed most of the aches and pains that the six weeks in the saddle had left in his body.

Reuben's was scoured clean of the trail dust and he headed in the direction of McMurrays Saloon. His right hand slipped easily across the butt of the Colt forty-five that was housed in the well worn holster on his hip.

The pistol was slid out of the holster in an unconscious movement. It was a habit that had grown on him over the years. It marked him out as a man to walk softly around to the old timers who had seen men like him before;

Flood was a gunfighter and more than likely, a killer, a man to avoid. Most men gave him nervous smiles and plenty of room.

After this week, Floods life would change. He was waiting for a herd of cattle that was being driven up from Juarez in Mexico. When that herd arrived bellowing and snorting onto El Paso's dusty street, the final chapter of his life as a hunter of men would come to a close.

The herd and its drovers had to cross the Rio Grande and they weren't due in El Paso for another six days, so until then he'd enjoy the delights of the town's whores, some good whiskey and the occasional game of Five Card Stud. These few luxuries were just part of a long list of pleasures that he had denied himself for the last ten years.

Now Flood was tired. He had become weary of a lifetime hunting down killers, rustlers and drunken thieves. His heart was heavy with the guilty deaths of more than a few innocent men who just happened to get in his way.

Flood had brought many men to the justice of the hang man's noose during a bloody career as a Bounty hunter. Those who had come peacefully rode behind him with their hands tied to the pommel of their saddles. The ornery ones that tried to escape were shot down and tied across their horses' backs.

It didn't matter to Flood whether they were brought back alive to be hanged, or dead, he got paid either way. He preferred dead, that way he wouldn't have to feed them on what was usually their final journey.

The cattle pens of El Paso were where he would meet the brothers. The Creed's were bringing a herd of longhorn cattle up from Mexico.

Flood pushed thoughts of the brothers into a corner of his mind. Sure in the knowledge that he would kill them, either face to face on the main street of El Paso or shot to death in the darkness of a back alley.

The time for vengeance was far enough away not to bother him for now, but in six days it would be back to business. His smile was grim and tight.

Back in Denver Colorado there had been an outstanding warrant since 1876 for Ethan and Seth Creed. The brothers had shot and killed a saloon keeper who had earlier thrown them out of his bar. That was just one of the many Warrants out for the Creed's.

They had sneaked back into the saloon under cover of darkness and shot Ollufson in the back. The lady who was keeping Matt warm that night took a bullet to her face when it had ricocheted off the bedroom wall.

She survived the bullet, but her ability to earn a living as a saloon girl was over. She still labours at Ollufson's saloon, but no money ever changes hands.

Martha Everett, once the most popular whore in Denver, now earns the right to sleep on the floor in Ollufson's backroom. Included in this payment is a half bottle of Wild Turkey whiskey, payment for keeping the Saloon floor and the spittoons clean.

She has slept by herself ever since the shooting. The bullet had taken away a thin slice of her left cheek. It caused her mouth to be set in a permanent sneer. These days Martha Everett couldn't give her body away for free.

The reward of Ten Thousand Dollars had been hanging over the brothers heads for all of them four years. The Creed's were wanted in a number of Southern States and Matt Ollufson's death was just one of the murders that they would pay for. Flood would make sure of that.

The Bounty hunter had come across a whiskey drummer more than a year since. He rewarded the man with five dollars for the information regarding the Creeds' whereabouts. The killers, a grateful salesman informed Flood, were working as cowboys on the Montoya ranch in Juarez Mexico.

With the seventy thousand dollars that he had on deposit at the First National Bank of Laredo, plus the guaranteed ten thousand dollar reward for the brothers, he would have enough to buy the Twisted Spur ranch from Kathryn Spillane. The Spillane ranch had just about the best grazing land in Colorado, and Flood wanted it.

Ever since the death of Jacob her husband, Mrs Spillane, or Kate as she preferred to be called, had made it known that she would sell the ranch to whoever came up with the Seventy five thousand dollars first. Well soon he would have that money and a bit to spare so that he would be able to restock what was left of Jacob Spillane's depleted herd. Then he could get out of the killing business.

The Creed's were killers, back shooters and then only under the cover of darkness. Flood had no qualms about killing them, he believed implicitly in the words from his mother's Bible, "*AN EYE FOR AN EYE.*"

The brothers would not face him in a gunfight, of that he was sure. They would try to bushwhack him, probably at night when he'd drank more than his share of McMurrays cheap whisky.

Flood had already made his mind up. He would shoot them down at the first opportunity and then present the local Sherriff with the reward notices. Then after his business with the brothers was done, Flood would be finished with killing men.

During the many years as a bounty hunter more than one faster gun had faced him, but it took a special kind of man to shoot another man down face to face. Flood was such a man. Men, who could beat him to the draw, froze for that heartbeat in time and they died in that second. He had learnt about so called fast guns a long time ago, if a man talked too much about shooting you down, then he usually hesitated for that split second. His nervous eyes would betray him and then he would end another man's life without a care. They needed to die and he needed the money.

Each cow town that he passed through yielded a little more information about the Creed's whereabouts. Now they were just a week away, driving a herd up from the Mexican border town of Juarez, to the cattle pens of El Paso. Then at last it would be over.

Reuben thought he would enjoy the nights in McMurrays saloon and then, for a couple of dollars he would have his bed in Gannon's, hotel warmed each night by one of El Paso's willing saloon girls

2

Martha

The out of tune plinking sound of a piano informed him that he was headed in the right direction. McMurray's sounded raucous. It was exactly what he wanted, there were bound to be friendly faces inside.

Cowboys and saddle tramps, eager for the company of people with the same outlook on life. Get drunk on cheap whiskey and then lose hard earned dollars to some card shark. If there was any money left and if the cowboy wasn't too drunk at the end of the night, then one of the saloon girls would relieve him of his last few dollars. In a week's time, when the cowboy was back on the trail, eating the dust from a herd of stinking steers, he would smile and remember what a great time he had had in El Paso. And he would look forward to doing it all again when the next cattle drive finished in three months time. That was the life of a cowhand.

*

Reuben smiled, and then grimaced. He remembered Martha Everett's face. She was just a small part of the reason he was here. Martha's maiden name before she had married Jacob Everett twelve years earlier was Flood. Martha was Reuben's older sister.

Jacob had died less than five years into the marriage, leaving Martha destitute with no money and no known family to care for her.

Martha Everett had then taken to make a living mostly on her back in Matt Ollufson's bed. There was no shame for Martha in what she had to do. She had done the same in Jacobs's bed for the near five years of a loveless marriage. Besides, Matt Ollufson was a kinder man. Not a bit like Jacob, who demanded what he saw as his right as a husband, that she was always available to him whenever he needed her. Even when he'd come home stinking of whiskey and saloon girls, which was most nights, Jacob Everett would satisfy his needs with whoever he gave the three dollars to.

Reuben was never much of a family man, but when the Creed's were dead and he was sure that taking them back alive wasn't an option, then he would take his sister to live with him on the ranch. He would put a roof over her head in return for her skill as a housekeeper; he knew Martha was a decent cook so that would be a bonus for the new ranch owner.

Flood was a straight forward business man. Living and dying were all just part of a brutal existence. Martha would understand that and after she had agreed to her brother's suggestion, then she would have a safe place to sleep. She would probably miss the safety of Matt Ollufson's bed, but that need would pass, it always did.

3

Maria

Another caress on the gun butt, and the grinning bounty hunter pushed against the bat wing doors of McMurrays Saloon.

The smell of unwashed bodies, cheap whiskey and stale beer greeted him as he elbowed his way into the crowded bar.

He flashed a toothy grin in the direction of four bored looking saloon girls who were sat at one of the card tables.

The effect was exactly as he'd expected. He was a stranger, probably with dollars in his pocket. The women, now brandishing wide smiles surrounded him. He ordered a bottle of Wild Turkey Whiskey from the bartender.

He awoke as dawn sunlight filtered through the wooden slats on the hotel window. Maria Lopez smiled at him. She had been watching him as he slept. Reuben smiled back at the woman, who had expertly eased a few more aches and pains from his lean body.

'Mister McMurray said you were probably a killer, a hunter of men, is that true Mister?' She smiled shyly at him again.

Flood gave the woman a sour look. 'It shouldn't matter much what I do for a livin' lady.' His eyes, cold and mean, caused Maria Lopez to flinch under his stare. 'Just as long as you get paid the three dollars for services rendered, I suggest you mind your business Ma'am.'

'I'm sorry mister; I didn't mean to pry into your business, I was just trying to make conversation.' Maria slipped an arm around his waist.

He allowed a smile back onto his face and pulled her close. For the next hour he enjoyed her body again.

Mostly Maria Lopez had fought like a mountain lion. She bit and scratched him, but when he asked if she was all right, she grinned through small white teeth. 'For sure mister gunfighter, you are the best lover I have ever had.' She dug fingernails into the flesh of his exposed back. 'What is your name mister?' Her words were forced through clenched teeth as she straddled him.

'Flood, Reuben Flood.' He was panting now. An idea was beginning to form in his mind, but he pushed it away until later. He met her thrusting body with his own instinctive lunges and the reason for his appearance in El Paso was lost for that hour in primeval lust.

4

Ethan and Seth Creed

During that week Maria Lopez and Flood spent all of their waking hours in McMurrays saloon. She watched him avidly as he won and lost hundreds of dollars at the card table.

He told her about the reason that he was in El Paso and that once the Creed brothers were handed over to El Paso's Marshall, he would head back to Colorado. There would be no problem collecting the reward once he showed the lawman the wanted posters for the Creed's, then it would be the long journey back home. Reuben was sick of this life; he needed to be away from killers and cattle thieves. He wanted the stench of death cleansed from his body.

Then during one hand of Poker, when the stakes were high and the card table was piled with ten and twenty dollar bills,

Flood froze momentarily; he had reached into his pocket for more dollars, when the distinctive rumbling sound rolled through the streets of El Paso. Flood grinned. He stood up abruptly and turning to Maria he threw a wad of bills onto the table. 'Finish the hand off for me Maria.'

There was no doubting that sound, a herd was being driven into the dusty town of El Paso. The Creeds had arrived a day early. His face was grim and he thought the brothers were probably good cattlemen. Maybe he would have ridden with them in another life. A picture of Martha's scarred face forced that thought from his mind and subconsciously his right hand flicked across the forty five on his hip.

Maria smiled and gathered up the dollar bills. 'Be careful Reuben.' She rubbed a hand across her face, remembering a painful encounter with one of the brothers. 'Ethan Creed is a brutal man.'

He gave her a puzzled look and then whispered. 'I know about the Creeds Maria. At the first sign of trouble I'll kill them both.'

Maria Lopez smiled, she knew this man was a killer of outlaws and the Creeds filled the bill on that score

The gamblers at the table relaxed. They were glad that the man whose hand kept fidgeting with the well worn butt of the forty-five on his hip was leaving. Reuben Flood made them all nervous.

A relieved gambler smiled at the Mexican woman who had taken Floods place at the table. She smiled back at him. Taking his money would be easy.

Reuben strode purposely through the batwing doors of McMurray's saloon and stared into a Texan sunset. The clouds that drifted across the evening sky were streaked with bloody red rays;

Flood shaded his eyes against the dipping sun. It was a warm evening, but his blood felt ice cold. His right hand slipped across the ivory handle of the forty- five, again.

The street was filling up with bellowing, thirsty and stubborn cattle. Flood watched in admiration as Mexican and American cowboys expertly herded the two thousand head of Longhorns into the cattle pens at the far end of town.

Half an hour after entering El Paso all of the drovers, caked in dust and cattle dung, began their joyful charge toward the saloon.

Reuben stood to one side as laughing men shouldered their way past him, eager for cold beer, hot women and cheap whiskey. All of which could be found inside of McMurrays saloon.

Flood grinned and thought the few girls in the saloon were going to be very busy, unless Zach McMurray could find a way to persuade some of El Paso's unattached ladies that for the next week or so, there was plenty of dollars to be earned by getting friendly with these cowboys. Men who probably wouldn't look too bad once they had been cleaned up and the right amount of dollars had changed hands.

Seth and Ethan Creed were the last two men through the saloons batwing doors. Neither paid any attention to the sour faced man who gave them icy stares as they shoved past him.

Ethan banged the leather saddle bag onto the bar. The cowboys fell silent as he began to count the silver dollars into stacks of ten. Then he called each man's name out and watched as they made their mark on the wage sheet.

Each cowboy made a whooping sound as he temporarily held on to his fifty dollar wages, most of which would disappear over the next few days, either in McMurray's cash draw, or more likely, into the purses of the saloon girls.

Seth made his way over to the poker game. His eyes widened in disbelief as he watched the Mexican woman, who he regarded as a whore, drag a pile of dollars from the centre of the table.

She had amassed maybe five hundred dollars in winnings. He leaned across the table and grabbed a handful of her jet black hair.

'What're doin' playin' cards bitch, where'd ya get the money from?' He turned and laughed in the direction of the cowboys who were filling dry bellies with Zach McMurray's beer and whiskey.

'You see this whore boys, she's usin' the money that she stole from us months ago. Then after spreadin' her legs she waited till we were asleep before riflin' through our pockets for the hard earned cash that we spent months eatin' dust for.'

He dragged the squealing Maria Lopez across the bar room floor, holding on to a handful of her black hair. 'Seems to me were all entitled to some of her profits, see'n as how we all made the original deposit.' Cackling laughter followed his ribald remark.

He threw the terrified woman in amongst the jeering cowboys. Their eager grubby hands searched under her red satin dress, they grasped and squeezed her flesh until she called out in pain. Seth reached for the pile of dollars.

'Creed,' Floods cold voice caused Seth's hand to hover over the money. 'They's my dollars boy and that's my woman you're hurtin.'

The bar dropped into a stunned silence, rowdy men waited for the inevitable killing. Seth Creed turned slowly to face the stranger.

'You're welcome to the whore mister, but the dollars belong to me and half the cowhands in this bar. This bitch here,' he pointed a dirt ingrained finger at Maria, who was trying to squirm under one of the tables for safety. 'Well she has emptied the pockets of all of these men at sometime or other, mostly when they were asleep.'

Heads nodded in agreement at Seth Creed's scornful words. 'Yeah,' a voice called out, 'that bitch took my last seven dollars while I was asleep, an' I want them dollars back, plus a little bit of interest, Waddya think ay boys.' Coarse laughter followed his words.

The voice became more confident. It found safety in the crowd who were all calling for some of the money that Seth had been about to pick up. 'Maybe a little bit extra for me an' the boy's heh Mex.' The cowboy bolstered by the Creed brothers bravado, strode across to the table that Maria was sheltering beneath and began to drag the screaming woman out by her ankles.

The booming sound of a pistol firing drowned out her screams. Her assailant pitched forward as Floods bullet slammed into his neck.

A deafening silence draped itself across McMurray's bar. Men shuffled in behind one another eager to be away from the gunman's cold stare.

Ethan Creed turned his head away from the last cowboy he had paid wages to. The hot silence of the saloon broken by the clicking of hammers on the shotgun that he'd left leaning against a chair. He aimed the barrel at Reuben's belly.

'An' who might you be mister?'

'Flood, Reuben Flood.' He stood watching Ethan, waiting for the tell tale sign in the drover's eye. The sign that said he was going to pull the triggers on the shotgun.

'Don't know you mister.' He swung the gun barrels over to where the woman was now standing at the bar. 'Why'd you want to help this whore anyway?'

'Like I told your cowboy, it's my money that she's usin.' His eyes narrowed to pinpoints of steel. 'And just so you understand me Creed, she is my woman.'

Ethan roared with laughter. 'You must be one of many saddle tramps who've fallen for this whore.' The jittery silence lifted as cowboys began to laugh at the stranger who laid claim to a woman that most of them had used for just three dollars on more than one occasion.

'Well you can have her pilgrim, be my guest.' Then he swung the gun barrel in the direction of Reuben's belly. 'Like I said, I don't know you stranger, so how'd you know my name is Creed?'

Flood flashed him a crooked toothed smile. 'Some years back you shot and killed a saloon owner up in Colorado, a feller who went by the name of Matt Ollufson.'

Ethan looked puzzled and then he slowly nodded his agreement at

Floods accusation. Seth Creed moved quickly to stand next to his brother.

'What's it to you mister?' Seth's hand hovered over the pistol at his hip.

He was about to pull the gun but his brother grinned and said, 'leave it Seth; I've got him covered, 'sides I want to hear what else he's got to say.' He reached behind him and picking up the whiskey bottle that the barman had set there when the cowboys had come in. Ethan gulped straight from the bottle neck. 'So go ahead Flood, finish your story.'

'When you two killers sneaked back into Ollufson's saloon that night, one of the bullets you fired at him, found its way into Martha Everett's face.'

'Jesus Christ mister,' Ethan creed spluttered. 'Are you the patron saint of all the saloon girls in America, she was just another whore for Crissakes.'

Once again McMurray's saloon echoed to the sound of cowboy's laughing. Even the bartender had produced a grin of disbelief, which disappeared quickly when Flood glared at him.

'Let's face it Creed.' Flood adjusted his stance. The fingers on his right hand were flexing at his side. 'You two have murdered quite a few men in your time. Mostly shot in the back and at night.'

The cowboys and the gamblers at the tables sensed the change in the brother's demeanour and began shuffling noisily toward the batwing doors.

'That woman back in Colorado was my sister, but she's not the reason I'm here.' From the pocket of his shirt he produced the wanted notices. 'Ten thousand dollars reward for you two killers.'

'You a Bounty hunter Flood?' Seth Creed sneered at him.

'Yep and it don't matter much to me whether you boys are dead or alive Creed, I'm takin' you both in.'

The forty-five appeared in his hand in a practised blur and Ethan Creed's right eye exploded as the bullet tore into his head, splattering brains over his brother's startled face.

The shotgun clattered to the floor. 'You murderin' bastard Flood.' Seth spat the words at the bounty hunter. He reached down for the shotgun.

Reuben shot him twice in the chest before Seth Creed's hand could grasp hold of the shotgun.

5

Leaving El Paso
Summer 1880

Marshall Bill Vogel gave the bounty hunter a sour look. 'You've completed your business here Mister Flood. The state of Texas will wire your blood money to the bank at Laredo.' The Marshall made sure that the bounty hunter clearly understood his next words. 'I don't much like your sort Flood. Your kind stinks of death and blood money and I'd be obliged if you and that woman of yours were out of my town before sundown.' His eyes squinted at the bounty hunter as he added the threat, 'or else you are going to have a big problem. Do you get my meaning mister?'

Reuben nodded and held his hand out to the lawman, but Vogel spat onto the dust-laden floor of his office, ignoring Floods outstretched hand.

Vogel spoke the next few words slowly. 'I see you again in El Paso Flood; I'll hang you for the murderin' bastard that you are.'

Reuben stared at Vogel's hard face. All of the lawmen that he'd come into contact with over the years were the same. They all hated him for the job he done, mostly because he was well paid for doing what they did for sixty dollars a month. Reuben knew if he stayed as a bounty hunter sometime or other a lawman would take great pleasure in shooting him down.

*

'Did you really mean that mister? What you said yesterday back there in the saloon.' Maria Lopez shielded her eyes from the morning sun with the Stetson she had bought in El Paso's only store. 'About me being your woman, was that true?'

'Wouldn't have said it if I didn't mean it Ma'am' He smiled at her and wiped away the first traces of sweat that had formed on his forehead.

'You know how I earn my livin' mister, goin' to bed with anyone who has the dollars to spend.' She shook her head in disbelief, waiting for him to tell her to ride on.

'We all have to make a dollar girl. And I think you've already got some of my dollars in your purse.' Grinning he turned in the saddle to face her. 'I've done worse for money, believe me Ma'am.'

El Paso's blacksmith had looked after Dan well. The roan's coat glowed under what must have been an hour's curry combing.

The horse whinnied its greeting to him as he strode into the forge after Marshall Vogel's no nonsense warning to him. He flipped the Smithy the promised gold Eagle and then he called into Finnegan's Livery stable, where he paid the proprietor fifty dollars from his poker winnings for a sturdy Bay mare. He hoisted Maria Lopez into the saddle and then the two outcasts headed along El Paso's dusty red street. They began the six week journey to Colorado.

'Most people think that what I do for a livin' is the worst kind of sin since Adam bit the apple.' Maria stared at him.

He grinned at her. 'Well Ma'am I think given the opportunity we can all change for the better. And I know it's going to be harder for me to give up my profession, than it will be for you to give up yours Maria.'

She didn't know anything about love, but she believed what she now felt for Reuben Flood must be close to it.

Maria stared at him as he led her through the barren land just about a mile out of El Paso. She smiled at his broad back and then she fought hard to stop the first tears she had cried since she had been a kid on the streets of Juarez.

Flood heard the stifled sob. He didn't turn to ask her why, he just gave Dan a kick in the ribs and the horse responded. The two horses began to eat into the first of the six hundred mile journey that would signal new lives for their riders.

He cast a final glance in the direction of the tree as the horses loped passed it. The tree was coming into its summer foliage, its branches full of shiny green leaves. Flood grinned. There was new life all around him; he hoped it was a good sign. His bloody past was beginning to fade.

Reuben's mind was now crowded with thoughts of the journey and the cattle he would buy. The beef would have his brand on their flanks. Right at the forefront of those thoughts was the uncomplaining woman who rode a couple of horse lengths behind him.

After the first week of hard riding, and the rations they had purchased, before Marshall Vogel had informed them that they were no longer welcome in his town, had been eaten and Reuben had to turn his hand to hunting for their food.

He shot mainly rabbits, but twice during the journey home he brought down a buck. He watched in morbid fascination as Maria skinned the animals. The knife she used was small, with a blade no longer than the trigger finger on his gun hand. Its cutting edge was honed bright and Maria worked silently and methodically. Each pelt was removed with expert flourishes of that wicked little blade.

'You're pretty good with that there knife Maria.' They were camped in a New Mexico canyon on the Colorado border, fifty miles from the ranch he would soon own when he paid Matilda Spillane her asking price.

'You had to be able use a knife like this Reuben Flood if you were not to starve in Juarez.' She lifted her eyes to his; the flickering flames of the fire gave her face a mournful look.

'My mother taught me how to use this knife when I was a little girl. I have skinned every kind of animal that there is. Mules, dogs, lizards, and snakes, even rats when there was nothing else to eat.' A single tear trickled down her sun reddened face and her mind resurrected some long ago memory from the hovel where she and her family lived across from the Rio Grande in the hot dusty and dangerous world of Juarez Mexico.

He stood up and joined the woman. Putting an arm around her shoulder Reuben pulled Maria close. A little tight smile passed over his face as he became aware that this was the first time he had ever shown affection to another person, usually old Dan was the only recipient of any care that the bounty hunter ever showed.

She pushed her head into his shoulder. Her voice was just a murmur. 'You have saved me Reuben Flood, saved me from the same fate as my mother and the other women in Juarez.' Her tears were flowing freely now.

He opened his mouth to speak, but Maria Lopez put a silencing finger to his lips. 'The women in my village mostly died from disease, or after giving birth to the children of nameless men who paid them a few dollars for their bodies. Some, like my mother were beaten to death by a husband in a Tequila drunken rage, because she had used the money that she had earned from some cowboy, to buy food for her children.'

Again she pulled herself closer to him and her voice became hard and emotionless. 'You have saved me from that life Reuben and for that I will always love you.' Then she sniffed loudly and somewhere out in the darkness beyond the glow of the campfires flames, a coyote howled its presence at the night. 'If anyone should ever hurt you, or try to take you away from me Reuben, I would kill them.' Reuben knew she was not just saying the words to impress him. The coyote howled again and he shivered.

He thought of the little skinning knife and a cold trickle of fear crept down his spine. Flood felt something for this woman, what it was he wasn't sure, but he would need a strong woman to help run the ranch. He figured Maria Lopez had that kind of hard bitten strength which he knew was missing from most of the men he had known. He grinned into the darkness of the night; it would make for an interesting conversation when Maria and his sister Martha met.

6

The Spillane Ranch

A month later the two riders entered Denver's busy main street. Reuben stopped at Ollufson's saloon. The saloon was now owned by a man named Mallory. The new proprietor had decided to keep the original name of the building. It had gained notoriety after the murder of Matt Ollufson and Mallory knew that any death caused by a gunfight was always good for business

Mallory had a notice put in the saloon window. "This bar is where the late Matthew Ollufson lost his life in a gunfight with the notorious Creed Brothers. There is a Ten Thousand Dollar reward for the capture of these lawless men." That crudely written epitaph always seemed to do the trick. The saloon was heaving with men full of bravado and cheap whiskey, each promising to hunt down the Creeds and claim the reward and the notoriety that would follow such a deed.

'I'm looking for Martha Everett.' Reuben spoke to the bartender.

The man gave Reuben a cursory glance and then jerked his thumb in the direction of a closed door toward the rear of the saloon. 'She's back there mister, but if you're looking for someone to keep you warm tonight, then the Everett woman don't do that no more.' He pointed to the group of saloon girls sat in the corner of the bar. 'I'm sure one of those ladies can help you.'

He finished the one way conversation with a smirk. Reuben's cold stare caused the man to begin an apology. Flood was already marching toward the back room, leaving the man's spluttering 'sorry' hanging in the air.

He dragged the startled woman out of Ollufson's saloon. 'Were all going home Martha.' He nodded in the direction of Maria, who was staring at the angry red scar on Martha's face. 'Me, you and Miss Lopez here.' Reuben nodded in Maria's direction. 'She's my woman by the way Martha. And we'd best make tracks; we've got a ranch to buy.'

Maria smiled at Reuben's sister. He had spoken to her about Martha and the scar on her face. Maria didn't think the scar was so bad, at least you can see her scars she thought.

The first few miles passed in silence, and then Martha asked Maria how she knew Reuben. By the time the Spillane ranch came into view the two women were engaged in earnest conversation.

It hadn't take Martha more than a minute to figure out how Maria had earned her keep back in Texas and soon the two women were swapping whispered tales of drunken cowboys who spent their hard earned dollars on women just like them. Sometimes a sniggering laugh would make Flood look around at his companions. This casual backward glance caused the women to fall into silence, for a few minutes anyway.

Reuben's spirit was lifted; his deadly past was beginning to fade as the three riders tied their horses to the hitching post outside Kathryn Spillane's run down ranch house.

Martha Everett hugged Reuben's woman. Maria thought of her new beginning, and something stirred inside her body. She hoped it was the new beginning which would tie Reuben Flood to her forever.

The deal for the ranch was completed when Kate Spillane put a bottle of genuine Scotch whiskey onto the ranch house table.

Reuben gave Kate Spillane his promissory note for the seventy five thousand dollars purchase price. The remainder of his savings would pay for an upgrading of the ranch house and the herd of cattle that came as part of the deal.

The new owner drained his whiskey in a single swallow and then he shook hands with a grateful Kate Spillane, who informed Maria and Martha that she was going back East to civilisation. Reuben smiled; he found it hard to believe that a man like him, a Bounty Hunter, could ever own a cattle ranch.

7

Nathan Flood
Colorado 1892

Martha Flood's smile was more of a frown them days. It was the best she could manage since Seth Creed's bullet had taken part of her face away sixteen years earlier. But as she had aged, the folds of skin seemed to hide the old scarring.

Martha had long ago forgotten Creed's laughing face when the killer had left her bedroom. Matt Ollufson was dead and she was bleeding like a stuck pig from the bullet wound across her face. It was a memory she had chosen not to visit again, why would she? Old scars are best left to themselves she thought.

After Reuben had married Maria, she had sobbed in self pity knowing that she would never have a man in her life ever again. She eventually put her life with Jacob Everett and Matt Ollufson into a corner of her mind, leaving it there gathering dust. She would never visit that part of her past again. Martha settled into a ranching life with more enthusiasm than she could have ever imagined.

Reuben was surprised but happy when she suggested that it might be a good idea if she took her maiden name back. And so Martha Flood was reborn. And the Spillane Ranch became the "Triple F Ranch."

Martha's face was wreathed in a crooked smile as she watched her eleven year old nephew swing the axe against an old oak tree's gnarled trunk. He'd been chopping at the oak for nearly two hours now and with just a few more strokes of the axe, Martha thought the tree would fall.

Nathan was half way to becoming a man, and she was proud of her nephew. He had the same lean build of his father, but that was all Reuben had given him. Everything else about him was pure Maria. Olive skin and almond shaped brown eyes. He was the handsomest boy she had ever seen.

The sky was beginning to darken and the clouds were thickening. Martha thought that it would snow quite soon. 'You're Ma sent me to tell you grub's up in ten minutes Nathan.'

He looked up at his aunt and grinned at her. Then Nathan swung the axe one more time. The tree finally gave up its resistance and old timber squealed in agony as it crashed onto the dry earth.

With snakelike agility Nathan dodged the falling tree and swaggered up to Martha. 'That should keep us in firewood this winter, don't you think aunt?' He stood a couple of inches taller than his aunt and she had to stretch herself slightly to kiss his forehead.

'Well done Nathan your father will be proud of you.' The boy hugged his Aunt and blushed at her praise.

Five hundred yards to the west of the "Triple F Ranch," two riders, one of them holding and old army spyglass watched as the woman and the boy disappeared into the ranch house.

Martha thought she had caught a glimpse of someone silhouetted against the darkening skyline, but heavy clouds had shrouded the fuzzy light. She tutted impatiently and blotted the image from her mind, the smell of roasting beef causing her mouth to water.

Reuben was sat at his desk, counting up the profits from this year's cattle sale. Martha smiled at him, but Reuben was engrossed in his figures. He didn't acknowledge her or the grinning boy who was waiting for a bit of praise from his father for the hours of work he had put into chopping down the oak tree.

They both knew better than to disturb him whilst he was doing ranch paperwork.

On many occasions Martha had shook her head in silent wonder when he was "doing the books" as he called his new job.

This once uncaring killer of lawless men for profit had confounded her and Maria by throwing himself into work that only ten years ago seemed impossible for him to consider as a way of life. She couldn't remember the last time she had seen the Forty-five strapped to his hip. The gun had been in a drawer of the desk that he had used for his paperwork for nigh on eight years.

By sheer hard work and bloody mindedness, Reuben had turned the Triple F into the most recognisable brand in the Colorado territory. The old ways were changing and Reuben was embracing that change.

Maria and Martha had worked hard. While Reuben was out buying and selling cattle, sometimes gone for a month or more, the two women carried out all the repairs on the ranch house which had been allowed to fall into poor repair during Matilda Spillane's last few years of ownership. In between cultivating a vegetable patch they took on the job of raising a boisterous Nathan Flood.

Now the boy was becoming a young man, and he took on all of the heavier tasks that had become more than his mother and aunt could handle. Reuben was slow with his praise for the boy. 'Let's just see what happens when he has to go out in the middle of a snow storm, to look for stray calves.'

Reuben grinned, 'Then we will see what the boy's made of.' But Maria and Martha knew that Reuben would walk through fire for his son.

On more than one occasion Maria had caught him staring at Nathan as the boy struggled to perform whatever task his father had set him that day. A tear would glisten in the old bounty hunters eye as Nathan refused to let himself be beaten by the difficulty of the task. Reuben had never helped his son to do something that he considered Nathan should be capable of doing, but when a particular job was finished, Reuben and his son would take off for the mountains and spend three or four days hunting and an unbreakable bond was formed between a proud father and a son who loved him. Nathan Flood was becoming a man in his father's image. Reuben's legacy would be safe in his son's hands.

Martha sat down at the huge oak table and beamed the best smile she could manage at Maria. Nathan's mother placed a dish with an enormous rib of roasted beef and a pan full of steaming potatoes into the centre of the table.

The meal was eaten with much appreciation of Maria's cooking skills. Reuben ruffled his son's jet black hair and then he kissed Maria on the lips and hugged Martha tightly.

Both women looked bemused by this very rare open show of affection. They knew that Reuben loved them all, but he wasn't normally the kind of man to show his feelings this way.

Then he went back over to his desk and produced a bottle of Wild Turkey whiskey from one of the desks many drawers. The bottle had been in the draw next to the pistol for at least a year.

'Good news for the ranch folks.' Reuben smiled at his family, 'We have made a near six thousand dollars profit during the last year.'

He placed four glasses on the old table and Reuben filled each glass to the brim. 'I think all of us deserve to have a drink to the success of the Triple F.'

Maria put a hand to her mouth, shocked by her husband's proposal. 'No drink for Nathan surely, he's only eleven years old Reuben?'

'He's more of a man than some that I've met and it's only one drink Maria. Nathan has worked hard like we all have, so one drink ain't gonna to do him no harm, is it boy.'

Nathan, not needing a second invitation, smiled sheepishly in the direction of his father and then he snatched the drink from the table. He swallowed the whiskey in a single gulp.

The fiery spirit scalded the boy's throat. Nathan coughed and spluttered as that part of the drink that didn't come down his nose, squirted between his lips and sprayed the floor at his mother's feet.

8

Lukas

When all the laughter had finished and he had swilled his burning throat with ladles of water from the barrel that was kept just outside the door, Nathan sat in embarrassed silence by the fireside; he tried hard to ignore his father's stifled laughter.

Martha had gone to fetch wood from the log store at the rear of the house and Maria, who had succeeded in controlling her urge urge for more laughter, had put a comforting arm around her son's shoulder.

The ranch house door banged open, allowing a swirling wind and the first snowflakes of winter to howl into the room.

'Don't you move, you murderin' son of a bitch.'

Reuben dropped the whiskey bottle to the floor and then reached for the gun that was always on his hip. Except it wasn't there anymore and it hadn't been there for years.

'Like I told you killer, you move one more time an' I'll splatter your insides all over that damn fireplace.'

A shotgun was levelled at Reuben's belly and it took him a few seconds to realise that the person holding the weapon was a woman.

She was dressed mostly in what looked like man's clothing to reuben. The clothes were old and shabby. Her boots were obviously years old and barely wearable. Beneath the battered Stetson, her straw coloured hair was filthy. The weapon was at odds with the way the woman looked. The shotguns double barrels glinted under the polish of gun oil. She meant business, both hammers on the shotgun were cocked and her hands were steady. She was going to kill him, of that he was sure. She could have been any age and Reuben searched his memory for a face, but came up with nothing.

'I don't know who you are lady, but I think you've made some kind of mistake here.'

She hawked phlegm from her throat and spat it into the fireplace. 'Like I said Reuben Flood, for sure you're a killer and there ain't been no mistake.'

She waved the gun barrel at Nathan and his mother. An' don't you go gettin' any ideas 'bout helpin' your daddy boy, cause' I'll kill you first an' you 'd do well to believe that boy'

Maria pulled Nathan tight to her body. The boy struggled against her grip, but Maria held him fast. 'Shush Nathan.' Her voice was trembling. 'There's been some mistake, she won't do us any harm, will you lady.'

The woman grinned through the few tobacco blackened teeth that she had left. 'First time I've ever been called a lady missus.' She swung the gun barrel back at Reuben's belly. 'An' like I told your murderin' dog of a husband here, there ain't been a mistake.'

Her voice was raised to a shout, 'Lukas, git yourself in here boy.'

He tramped into the room. A boy maybe three or four years older than Nathan stood and stared at the frightened woman and her son.

Reuben flinched, and then his eyes wandered to the desk draw that held the colt. He wouldn't make it. This crazy bitch would blow him away before he got halfway to the desk. *Best to wait* he thought *for the explanation he knew was coming.* His brain searched for a solution.

He'd come across would be killers like this before. A little grin appeared on Floods face. They always wanted to tell you why they were going to kill you, instead of just shooting you down. And they always lost the edge, his chance would come, it always did.

The boy was dressed in similar poor worn out ragged clothes that the woman wore, obviously handed down from an elder brother, or even a father. His face was hidden by the Stetson that was jammed down over his eyes. He held an army issue pistol at his side.

'That's him there Lukas.' Her voice was cold. She raised the shotgun to Reuben's head. 'I've waited best part of twelve years for this moment.' The woman directed her voice to where Maria was sat, her arms tight around her son's shoulders.

'My name Missus Flood is Leila, Leila Creed, an' you are the Mexican whore that was in McMurray's saloon the night Flood here shot my boys'

The boy raised a shaky hand until it was level with his shoulder and pointed the weapon at Reuben's head.

'Not yet Lukas, I'll tell you when boy.'

Maria remembering that awful day, hissed at the woman, 'If Reuben hadn't killed those two back shooting cowards, then I would have.'

Leila Creed ignored the angry Mexican woman and spoke directly to Reuben. 'See this boy here bounty hunter. This is my Seth's son an' it was you that shot and killed his daddy.'

Reuben allowed his eyes to wander back to the kid. *He was the weak link.* If he could get close to the nervous looking boy, then maybe he had a chance.

He turned back to the woman. Flood knew it was no good trying to bargain with her, but if he could distract her for long enough, then he'd make a play for the kid's gun and then he'd kill the crazy bitch and if needed, the kid would die as well.

Maria's gasp caused Reuben to twist around to face his wife. 'Santa Maria.' She covered her face with shaking hands. 'Satan has come to claim us.' She pointed a finger at the boy.

Lukas Creed had removed the battered Stetson from his head. Matted white hair hung down against the skin of the boy's pure white face.

'His eyes Reuben look at his eyes.' Maria was pointing at the scruffy boy who was aiming a gun at her husband.

Flood had seen all kinds of crazies in his time as a hunter of men, but this thing in front of him made his blood run cold. The boy's hair hung down in dirty white strands. Behind the greasy strands of hair, watery pink eyes kept an unwavering stare on Reuben's stony features.

Leila Creed spoke in hushed tones, 'This boy is special, he's what you call an Albino, an' he's a gift from the Lord God hisself.' Then she turned to her grandson 'Well now you have seen him Lukas, the man who murdered your Daddy. He don't look so tough now does he boy?'

As the old woman's words died away, the gun in Lukas Creeds fist bucked twice. The first bullet smashed into the shoulder of a surprised Reuben. The second bullet took him high in the chest.

Reuben's knees buckled and the one time bounty hunter slipped onto the rough wooden boards of the ranch house floor.

'Okay boy.' Leila Creeds words were full of pride. 'Git yourself outa here, I'll take care of these people. Then I'll meet you back at the cabin in a couple of days.'

Lukas grinned at the stunned Maria and then disappeared through the open cabin door which led out into increasingly heavy snow flurries.

Maria screamed Reuben's name and ran across the room to her stricken husband. She cradled his head in her lap.

Reuben blinked his eyes at her and then a weak smile crossed his lips. Maria thought she heard him mumble the words "I love you."

His face was strangely beautiful in death Maria thought, and then she kissed his pale lips.

Leila Creed backed out of the cabin door, snowflakes whirled around her head. 'First one of you that sticks a head outa this door gets it blown clean off. And that goes for you to boy.' She spat again, this time onto the wooden floor. 'Your Daddy has paid for the murder of Lukas' Daddy boy, now let that be an end to it.' She turned and disappeared from the tear filled eyes of Maria Flood into the night's increasing snow flurries.

Martha Flood had dropped the cut logs onto the snow covered ground when she had heard the gunshots. She had listened in silence at Leila Creed's venomous threat to her sister in-law and as Leila had come crashing out of the cabin door, Martha slammed the short handled axe into the fleeing woman's forehead. Then she screamed her brother's name into the night sky.

9

El Paso.
November 1913

Maria had taken the stage coach to Santa Fe where she purchased a Bay mare from a nearby ranch. The horse would take her the last two hundred miles.

She preferred riding the horse; it had in Maria's mind turned the two week journey into a pilgrimage. The time had arrived and that long ago past needed to be revisited.

Maria Flood had told Martha that she needed to find what was left of her family down in Juarez Mexico.

Reuben's sister had shrugged her agreement at Maria, but she wasn't convinced by her sister-in-law's need to make the twelve hundred mile round trip to visit a family who were probably all dead by now.

Maria could have taken the train, but she felt at home with the horse. Riding in a railway coach behind a smoke belching monster filled her with dread.

El Paso had changed. The landscape during last ten miles of her ride was dotted with the strange contraptions that she knew had something to do with getting oil out of the sun baked earth.

Texas was different now. Her life was all about cattle and open range.

El Paso it seemed was jammed full with the new and very rich oil prospectors, along with what seemed like thousands of get-rich-quick conmen that boom towns always attracted, Maria smiled grimly and thought that in her other life she would have taken full advantage of a town overflowing with rich men. But now she hated this new America and when her business was done here, she would overcome her dreaded fear and take the train home. Maria hoped that she would be long dead before the new America came knocking at the ranch door.

Her son was a full grown man now and the ranch was thriving. He had secured a contract with the rail company to supply beef to rail workers. It wasn't long before new towns had grown up along side of the steel tracks that were cutting through America's west and ranch owners were becoming rich, feeding on the changes that she feared.

Her son was no different to any of the other ranchers. He was the future and Maria knew that the First National Bank of Colorado was holding a million of her family's dollars. Oil and steam had become the future and Maria Flood along with her family would be a big part of that future

She dismounted the Mare at El Paso's livery. Surprised that there was still a business for horses in what was now a booming oil town. The noise shocked her. Yes there were still people riding horses along the mud street, but there were as many of the new world's latest craze, motor driven smoke belching vehicles.

The noise and the stench of oil and filth invaded her senses and she reeled under that assault.

She hurried along the wooden sidewalk and smiled her appreciation for this little bit of progress. The sight of McMurrays Saloon made her stop and gasp. It was huge now. At least three times the size of the original building.

The noise of a piano and raucous laughter pulled at an old memory and she had to fight of the urge to push through the old batwing doors.

The woman carried on past Gannon's hotel, which had also outgrown its original size and it boasted a huge sign above its fancy new entrance. She shook her head sadly. Maria Flood preferred the slums of Tijuana to the streets of today's El Paso's. She was sure

Satan walked this towns raucous streets..

This part of the world, where once she and scores of women just like her, plied their trade as saloon girls, frightened her now. When her business was done in El Paso, she would leave it again, never to return.

Maria read the words on Gannon's gaudy sign.

Welcome to Gannon's first class hotel.
Come and sample the delights of our dancers.
Enjoy Real French Champagne.
You are the state of Texas' new prosperity.
Don't waste your dollars in lower class hotels.
We have everything for hard working American oilmen.

Gannon's was bursting at the seams with oilmen and garishly

dressed women who claimed they were as French as the Champagne that their customers consumed in huge quantities.

She shook her head, parts of El Paso were still recognisable, but they were being swallowed up by scores of offices all offering to take the money and return huge profits to the fortunate investor. A thousand dollars was the minimum investment and that could turn you into a millionaire within a year.

Judging by the twenty dollar cost for a bottle of genuine French Champagne on offer at Gannon's first class hotel, she thought that only millionaires could survive in West Texas.

Maria grimaced at the sign and hurried on down what appeared to be a new wooden sidewalk. The woman could see the sign for the office that she had been looking for.

The sign was big and in brash red lettering, just like all of the others that were touting for business.

The El Paso Oil Company.

A minimum investment of One Thousand Dollars required
Don't miss out on the Texan oil boom.
We guarantee huge returns.

She dismissed all of the information; it was only the name of the office manager at the bottom of the sign that interested her. Maria pushed the heavy wooden door open and was surprised by the lush interior. All of the furniture was fashioned from oak and it glowed under a layer of polish. Not like the rough carpentry of the ranch she grimaced at the obvious waste of time and money. The office walls were covered with sepia colored pictures of stern faced men dressed in tailored suits.

'Howdy Ma'am. Welcome to the El Paso oil company.'

The voice startled her, Maria turned to face the man who had entered the office through a door at the far end of the room.

'Sit yourself down in that there chair Ma'am and let me show you how to become rich.' His voice was wrapped up in a big friendly laugh. 'You are looking to invest ain't you Ma'am?' She nodded at him and he guided her to a huge leather chair.

She felt tiny and vulnerable, the chair seemed to swallow her slight body.

He was tall maybe six-six she thought. A huge gut hung over the leather belt that held his pants up.

At first glance he could have been the wrong man. But the hair, long and pure white, was tied up at the back in a horse's tail. Maria shivered, she had found him.

He grinned at her and she trembled. She couldn't see his eyes, he wore a pair of new fangled spectacles with dark blue lenses, but it was him, of that she had no doubt. She fought hard to stop herself from crying out.

He sat down on a fancy leather swivel chair and he spun it around so that he faced the desk. Then he took a handful of papers from an open draw in the highly polished piece of furniture. 'My name is Creed Ma'am, Lukas Creed and can I ask, are you a Mexican Ma'am?' His question was laced with sarcasm.

Her reply was edged with anger. 'Yes mister Creed I am, is there a problem with that?'

'No Ma'am, aint no problem at all, it's just that we don't get many of your kind in here with spare dollars to invest. But as long as you have got the money, El Paso Oil really don't care where you come from. Now if you could just give me some details.' His massive shoulders shook just a little as he choked back a small laugh.

Creed's broad back seemed to take up all of her vision; she felt sick, a little trickle of fear crept down her spine. He seemed to sense her anxiety, his next words were soft, he was eager to put a potential customer at ease 'You won't regret going with El Paso Oil Ma'am, all of our investor's are guaranteed to make a healthy profit.'

She bit at her lower lip and Maria's heart pinged in a tight chest. 'I'm sure of that mister Creed. El Paso Oil looks like an extremely prosperous business.'

'Yes Ma'am, we are the biggest and surely best of the oil companies which have grown up in the last ten years; your dollars are safe with us Ma'am. Now can I have your name please?'

She reached into the valise and moved a little coil of rope to one side; Maria clasped sweaty fingers around the butt of Reuben's pistol. 'Maria, Maria Flood.'

Lukas Creed stiffened in the chair. He didn't turn around.

Maria heard the whispered curse and In spite of her fear, she glided silently across the space between them. The old gun felt almost too heavy in her hand. 'I've come to put an end to some unfinished business.' Her words were strong and full with more than twenty years of venom. She swung the butt of the gun at his head. Maria flinched as the gun crashed against the back of his skull.

He slumped forward in the chair and his forehead smacked onto the desk. A groan slipped from the unconscious man's slack mouth and the woman quickly overcame her revulsion of Reuben's killer. She worked silently, using the coil of rope from the valise to tie him into the chair.

After a few minutes he moved. Creeds head had lolled to one side. His voice was muggy. 'So you're still alive then whore?' His voice mocked her just like his grandmother's had all those years ago. His tied hands making grasping gestures at the open drawer that he had taken the investment papers from.

She thumbed the hammer back on the pistol. The click of the gun being cocked jerked him upright.

'You won't shoot me bitch; you're just another Mexican whore who robbed cowboys of their wages whilst they slept.'

She leaned across him, careful to avoid his watery pink eyed stare; she removed his tinted spectacles. Then Maria, just as she had done more than twenty years earlier, gasped in horror when the young Lukas Creed had removed his battered old Stetson. She repeated the same words again to the blessed virgin. 'Santa Maria, it really is Satan himself.'

'So bitch, now that you have got me trussed up in this chair what are you going to do next? Steal my money, just like you did when you robbed all of them poor cowboys; I should have shot you as well as that murderin' bastard of a bounty hunter that you were married to.'

Creed's voiced sliced into her brain and she flinched under his savage words and the mocking watery eyed stare. Her hand went back into the valise at her feet and she pulled a neckerchief from the bag's open top.

He moved his head violently from side to side as she tried to force the cloth into his mouth. Creeds teeth gnashed together as he tried to bite her fingers.

The pink eyes were wet with angry tears as he glared at her. 'You won't shoot me bitch, this office would be full of lawmen within seconds of any gunfire.' He grinned at her and then spat into the woman's face.

Eventually she jammed the cloth into his mouth and he gave up the struggle. Lukas Creed was safe in the knowledge that the bitch might do him some damage, but she wouldn't kill him. And when he was freed, and he had no doubt that he would be freed by some lawman, or maybe a potential investor looking to make a fortune out of the Texan oil that was going to change the world. Then the whore would pay for this little episode, but not quick like that murderin' bastard that she had married. No sir, she might be pushing fifty he thought, but she was still a good looker, for a Mexican whore.

When he had finished with her, then she would die real slow. In spite of the gag in his mouth Creed managed something that resembled a smile and Maria Flood slumped back into the leather chair. She shrank into the chair's hugeness. The woman trembled with fear and hatred for this man who she considered to be the devil.

Creed stared at her; he gained strength and satisfaction from her dilemma. Whether she should shoot him down, just as he would if he was in her position, or to flee and try to escape his bloody revenge. He closed the pink eyes and contemplated how he would end her life.

She stood up quickly and dropped Reuben's gun into the valise, then after putting a shaking hand into the bag, Maria stumbled back over to her captive.

He opened his eyes again and smiled at her. Maria spun the chair around so that Creed faced the pictures of the oil millionaires that gazed fiercely down at whoever ventured into their offices.

Maria waved the wicked blade in front of Lukas Creed's startled eyes.

'It's a skinnin' knife Mister Creed, I'm sure you recognise it. Your old dead grandmother probably had one just like it.'

Realisation of his fate dawned on the oil man and he began to jerk wildly in the chair. But in a swift movement she had already slashed the back of his neck. The skin parted into six inch long gash.

Lukas Creed's body trembled in shock. Then with another swift movement of her hand, she drew the little blade up through the rolls of fat in his neck and across the top of his head, stopping the slicing cut just between the devils eyes.

Maria halted her grisly task just long enough to slide the bolt across the door. She tested the door handle and satisfied it was locked, she drew the heavy curtains together. Then she went to work silently, with only the eyes of old dead oilmen to witness her sin.

An hour later she left the Texan Oil Company office and made her way to the single platform at El Paso's new railway station.

Maria could hear the whoop of a train's steam whistle. She felt strangely calm as the train came to a halt next to the empty platform. She would be the train's only boarder.

Within a minute of the train grinding to a halt, hundreds of passengers left the smoke belching giant and crowded onto the platform. Maria climbed the iron steps, and made her way to a seat in the near empty carriage. A sour grin clouded her face. 'I'm the only one leaving El Paso today, these poor deluded folk are hoping to make their fortunes in this God forsaken town, well good luck to them, they're going to need it'

The voice of a sad faced porter informed the few passengers who were left on the train 'The next stop is Santa Fe.' She felt the engine strain and lurch into life. A few minutes later the rocking motion of the train had sent her into a troubled sleep.

Images of Lukas Creed stared at her through watery eyes and more than once on the ten hour journey, Maria Flood cried out in terror as she relived the bloody nightmare in the office of the Texan Oil Company

The few other passengers in the carriage ignored her garbled cries, preferring to sleep their way through the cold journey.

The train pulled into Santa Fe; Maria Flood called at the Broken Spur ranch and bought a roan mare from the ranch foreman. Then she began the three week ride back to Denver.

*

Many months later, when Law men from the Pinkerton Detective agency had eventually interviewed some of her fellow travellers, none of them could remember having seen anyone that might have resembled a killer hurrying from a gruesome murder. It seemed to the Pinkerton men that the gruesome killer would never be found.

10

Colorado Territory
January 1914

Maria had eventually become aware that she was back on Triple F land, when her galloping horse scattered a grazing herd of Longhorns. All of the steers bore the Triple F brand burnt into their rumps. Mixed in with the Longhorns were several distinctive Hereford calves.

She smiled. Her son's experiment with Hereford bulls, imported from

England was paying off. Reuben would have been proud of Nathan's achievement.

The joy that she felt in being back on the land that Reuben, Martha, herself and the son who Reuben had cherished more than his own life, had turned into probably the most successful ranch in the state of Colorado, was now overshadowed by the nightmare of El Paso. It was a self inflicted horror and she would carry it with her for the rest of her life.

The raw nights were spent huddled under a blanket around a blazing campfire, terrified of sleep. And always the same dream would invade her mind.

She had slipped the skinning knife under the skin at the back of Lukas Creed's neck and then she began to peel his flesh away from the bone of his skull. The muffled screams were only silenced when his body had become rigid with shock. The skin came away from bloody sinew and her heart almost stopped at the sight of the pink bulging eyes that glared at her from the bloodied skull Maria spat into what was once a face, but was now just a gory mess.

An hour had passed and when it was over Maria Flood said a prayer to the Blessed Virgin, who she knew was not listening.

*

She awoke from the nightmare, screaming for forgiveness from Christ's mother. The only creatures to hear that prayer were the animals that had crept close to her smouldering campfire during the bitter coldness of the night. They scattered at the sudden interruption to their foraging, back to the safety of the scrub land that surrounded her makeshift camp and eventually to disappear into Colorado's darkness. Only the howl of a solitary coyote remained, echoing in the darkness.

The woman shivered as the animal's mournful wail hung in the crisp air above her campsite. Of all the sins she had committed in the past, the brutal slaying of Lukas Creed would haunt her for the rest of her life. There was no escape from that horror.

She had wanted to kill the man who had taken her man's life. Reuben had lifted her from the whorehouses of West Texas and had made her feel wanted and loved. She had given the bounty hunter a son and a solid reason to hang up his guns.

The triple F ranch had prospered. Maria had spent many a night sitting on the rough wooden bench that Reuben had made all those years ago, staring up at a sky filled with a million stars. She had no idea what use the stars were, but she knew that somehow God had made them for her and Reuben Flood, the man who had rescued a Mexican whore from the cesspit of El Paso. In all the years of their marriage, Reuben had never once mentioned her past life and she had loved him more for that omission.

Martha, Reuben's sister, who had also made a living from selling her body, embraced Reuben's wife. The two women had many times swapped lurid tales of cowboys caked in trail dust, with pockets full of dollars and nights of drunken debauchery.

At least her sister in-laws scar was visible. The scar that Seth Creeds bullet had left on Martha's face could still just about be seen. But as she had aged, the folds of skin on her cheek had covered it up. Maria's scars were all inside and now they were tearing her apart.

She stared down from the ridge just as she knew Leila Creed had done all those years ago. Maria could see smoke drifting up into clouds that were beginning to blot out the stars. She was sure it would snow by morning.

The final week of her journey had been littered with ever increasing snow falls. Soon this part of Colorado would become an impassable white wilderness.

Maria unsaddled the horse and tied the dangling reins to the bare branches of a bush. Then she set about making a fire. Looking down at the ranch that had been her home for more than twenty years, she gulped back tears as the smoke, from the stove in the house that she shared with her sister in-law and Reuben's fine son, curled slowly up into a sky that was swiftly being covered with snow laden clouds.

She would never go back to the ranch. Maria felt the weight of the murder, for that's what Lukas Creeds death was, a cold blooded murder. How could she go back to a life with her son and Martha with that sin burrowing into her soul?

Tomorrow she would go back to Texas and face whatever justice her God had set out for her.

This hard ground which overlooked the Triple F ranch far below would be a more comfortable bed than the one she had slept alone in since Reuben's barbaric death.

She laid the sheepskin from her bedroll up against a sheltering boulder. It would be a bitterly cold night; Maria Flood accepted the oncoming snows as the beginning of a hard penance.

The horse whickered and stamped a foreleg, trying to get her attention. She scowled at the animal. It needed feeding but food for both horse and rider could wait, she needed to build a fire. Her hands and fingers were starting to numb. 'Later horse;' her voice trembled as the snow whipped by the freezing wind slashed across her face, 'you will be fed later when I can get some heat into my body.'

The wind howled through her campsite; and drifting snow was beginning to pile up against the boulders that were dotted around her camp. She stared up at the snow laden sky and she whispered prayer that the snowfall would cease long enough until she was far away from Colorado territory.

Tomorrow after some hot coffee and a breakfast of dried beef, she would ride to Denver's rail station and take a train to Texas, Hoping to find some kind of salvation.

But for now Maria needed sleep. The one way trip back to El Paso would be yet another part of her never ending nightmare, even in the relative shelter of a steam train's carriage.

Dreams filled with Lukas Creeds bloody face, faded to be replaced with images of her brothers and sisters dressed in rags playing happily on the filthy streets of Juarez.

She smiled in dreamy contentment. Maybe she would go straight back to Mexico. A life on the streets of Juarez was all she deserved. The sleeping woman was accepting of her fate.

The horse shifted uneasily and then she heard the sound, the unmistakable tread of a horses hooves crunching against the snow.

Maria's hands scrabbled for the rifle that was tucked into her bedroll. Then the horse and its rider crashed through the brush that surrounded her camp. The Winchester fell from Maria's grasp and her legs began to tremble uncontrollably.

The riders face was covered by a heavy woolen scarf and a black

Stetson was jammed tight over hidden eyes.

Maria's hands clawed at her own frightened face. The horse towered above her. It was him, the ghost of Lukas Creed on the animal's back, come to exact a bloody revenge for her crime.

She screamed her contrition at the rider. 'I'm sorry for what I did to you.' Then Maria threw herself onto the snow-covered ground. Her voice was shrill as she pleaded for Creed's forgiveness.

'It's me Maria, are you all right?' The Stetson was pulled from the rider's head and the weeping woman recognised her sister- in-law's voice; it was Martha.

'I saw the smoke from a fire late last night and I decided to check it out this morning. Why didn't you come down to the ranch instead of nearly freezing yourself to death up here?'

'I need to go back to Texas Martha; I have done a terrible thing.'

'I know what you did Maria.' Martha dismounted from her horse and helped the distraught woman to her feet.

'No you don't Martha, you can't know.'

Martha put an arm around Maria's shoulder and hugged her dead brother's wife. 'I thought it was strange that you would go back and visit your family after all these years.'

Maria tried to protest, but Martha shushed her. 'I went into Denver last week, before the snows set in, to get some supplies for the winter and I overheard some of the townswomen gossiping in Brad

Calder's store.' Martha's eyes glistened with tears. 'It seems that one of their husbands is the telegraph operator and he had received some information on the wire about a man who had been skinned alive in an office down in El Paso.'

Maria buried her head in Martha's shoulder as huge sobs racked her body. She already knew what Martha's next words would be.

'The man had pink eyes and long white hair Maria, It was him wasn't it, the Creed boy, him that shot and killed your Reuben?'

'Yes Martha and now I've got to go back to El Paso.' Maria's sobbing had ceased. 'I've got to pay for my sin Martha, every time go to sleep I can see those eyes staring at me.'

'No Maria, you don't have to go back. Lukas Creed shot Reuben to death and for that he deserved to die so let that be an end to it all.'

'But not the way I killed him Martha. I skinned him like a critter and that can't be right. God will never forgive me for that.'

'That's for you and your God to sort out Maria.' Martha held her sister-in-law close. 'But we have got a ranch to run, and you have got a son and as big as the boy is, he still needs his Ma to look after him.' She could feel the Mexican woman sobbing again. 'He's lost a father; don't take his mother away from him Maria.'

Maria wiped her tears away with the back of her hand and nodded her agreement to Martha. 'One thing Martha, Nathan must never know what I've done, I don't want Reuben's boy to know that I'm a brutal murderer just like that son of a bitch Lukas Creed.'

'He'll never know from me Maria, And you know something, there are lots of men who have been killed down in Texas. It's a God forsaken place, and Creed's death will become just a part of the hell that an oil town like El Paso has become.'

Martha walked over to where Maria's horse was tied to the scrub bush and then she held the horse's reins out to her. It's time to go home Maria Flood. 'Sides young Nathan will be gettin' home soon an' he'll be lookin for his Ma.'

The ride back down to the ranch house was completed in an awkward silence. Maria could not shake the feeling that there was something else to say.

*

Martha spoke in a hushed voice to her nephew. 'Your Ma is in a bad place Nathan. She don't know it was you that brought the news about Creed's skinnin' so you just be quiet boy and let your Ma live out her years in peace.'

Martha's hands caressed Nathan's head. 'Your daddy would have let it go Nathan. He would have made sure that we kept this place and made it work boy. And for now the Triple F needs your Ma. So just you think on before you open that boy's mouth of yours.'

Nathan nodded an agreement to his aunt and then a grim faced Martha began to set the evening's food out on the table that Reuben Flood had nailed together more than twenty five years earlier.

Maria held Nathan close to her breast, remembering when he

would snuggle close to her as an infant and feed on her precious milk.

'Everyone okay down in Juarez Ma?'

'They're all fine son, now you eat this good food that you're Aunt Martha has cooked up for us.' The lie came easily to Maria Flood's lips; she had not set eyes on any of her family since Reuben had taken her from the streets of El Paso more years ago than she cared to remember. She pushed the lie away and hid it in a dark crevasse deep in her mind, along with the horror of Lukas Creed's skinned body.

The meal passed in silence. Maria looked up from the plate of food that she was trying hard to swallow, she caught her beautiful son looking at her through sad eyes and Maria Flood had no doubt that Nathan

Flood, Reuben's fine boy, knew her gruesome secret. She began to weep.

'It doesn't make a difference how Lukas Creed died ma, he was a killer an' he deserved his fate.'

'But not like that Nathan, not skinned like some animal.'

Tears streamed down Maria Flood's cheeks. 'I should have let the law deal with him son. He would have been tried and then hanged, like all murderers. Just like what they'll do with me Nathan.'

'No ma that ain't never gonna happen. You done what were right. Dad would have killed him any way that he could. So let's just concentrate on this ranch ay Ma.' His voice was clinical 'Times are changin' fast and I'm going to need you and Aunt Martha to help run this ranch Ma.' He drank a mouthful of scalding coffee.

'I read in the paper that Europe may be at war soon and maybe us Americans could get involved in it. If a war does begin Ma, lots of American men will join the army. Armies need feedin' Ma. And I intend that the Triple F ranch will be the main supplier of beef to the American army.'

Nathan's eyes took on a hard flinty stare. 'There is a fortune to be made out of cattle Ma and I intend that we are going to get our hands on as much of it as we can.'

Maria shivered at her son's cold words. He was Reuben's son alright, He had the same bloody mindset that his father had had when chasing outlaws down and then killing them for money.

She had no doubt that Nathan would succeed and become a rich and powerful landowner. Maria's thoughts took her back to the Texas of more than thirty years ago, when she had sold her body for a few dollars and she nodded her acceptance at Nathan's words. You do what you have to, just to stay alive.

After the food was eaten, Nathan sat at his father's desk and completed the day's paperwork.

11

1918
Triple F Ranch

Martha rummaged through the draws of Reuben's old desk. She grinned as her fingers wrapped themselves around the neck of a whiskey bottle. Then she went outside and sat next to Maria on the porch of the ranch house. They spent the next hour reminiscing a long ago past.

Mostly the old women laughed at the memories of whore houses frequented by Cowboys and Snake oil salesmen whose pants pockets were bulging with dollars, until they had spent their money and all of their energy in a raucous week of drunken debauchery. Then they would be gone for another three or four months, eating the dust of the next herd that was bound for the slaughter houses of El Paso.

Martha turned to her sister –in-law. Maria heaved a sob. 'I'm sorry Martha; I just remembered Reuben and that damned horse ride from El Paso. He made me, a saloon girl, feel so special.'

And then Maria also recalled the horror of a return journey to El Paso, ending with her sadistic killing of Lukas Creed. She buried her face into the palms of her hands.

'You're thinkin' about that bastard Lukas Creed ain't you Maria?'

'Yes Martha, I am. And I don't think that nightmare will ever go away.'

'Remember what I said to you all them years ago Maria. One day we will all pay for our sins, everyone does. Until then just you think on Nathans words.' She pulled Maria close to her. 'Lukas Creed, he said was a murderer. An' so were the rest of his family. And it don't matter much how you die Maria, just so you pay in the end.'

She looked up at Martha. In the flickering lantern light it was hard to see the scar on Reuben's sister's face now, but Maria knew it was still there. Like all secrets, it was hiding just below the surface, waiting for someone to peel back the skin.

'Yes Martha, you're right. Reuben took two women out of filthy whorehouses and gave them a good life. For that alone I will grateful. And I pray to the Blessed Virgin every night that she will keep my son safe.'

Martha smiled at her. 'Y'know Maria, that damn war in Europe ain't gonna last much longer Maria. The newspaper feller in town, you know him, Matt Gibson I think his name is, well he told me it'll be all done by Christmas. And then our boy will be back home where he belongs, runnin' the Triple F Ranch.' Martha laughed. 'Sides someone has got to look after us two old saloon girls ain't they Maria?'

Maria's thoughts once again travelled back across the years to Juarez in Mexico, where kids played outside the filthy hovels that passed for homes. Then she thought of the grandchildren that Reuben would never see. Tears streamed down her face.

After wiping her cheeks dry, Maria smiled back at Martha. Reuben would live on through the ranch he had bought from Kathryn Spillane. Now she hoped her husband's legacy would become a big part of his son's future.

'Hey Maria look, lights?' Martha had stood up and was pointing to the flickering of lights that were travelling along the road which led to the ranch house. 'I think it's one of them new fangled motor things that some feller from back East invented'

Five minutes later the Ford motor car came to a rattling halt in front of the two curious women.

Nathan Flood stepped out of the car and then he walked around to the passenger side and opened the door.

A woman, almost as tall as Nathan, eventually struggled through the vehicles open door.

'Mother, Aunt Martha, I want you to meet Eloise Baptiste. We met six months ago in Paris and we're going to get married.'

Maria pointed to the woman's swollen belly. 'Best make the wedding quick then ay Nathan. From the looks of Miss Baptiste's belly there, the child ain't gonna be much longer in comin' is it boy?' Then she ran to her son and smothered his face in kisses. Maria whispered her tearful prayer of thanks to the Blessed Virgin for her beloved sons return.

After much fussing around of the very pregnant French woman, Martha spent a few minutes searching through the draws in Reuben's old desk, again. She eventually found another bottle of her brother's whiskey.

Each of them raised a toast to the merging of the two soon to be members of the Flood family, or the new dynasty as Nathan called it.

The whiskey sent everyone to bed in a buoyant mood.

Maria raised a disapproving eyebrow as her son and the slightly drunk Eloise commandeered her bedroom. Martha laughed raucously before informing Maria that she had been usurped as the most important woman in her son's life now. 'It looks like it's the chair in front of the fire for you Gal, or, you can share my bedroom if you like.' Again Martha laughed. 'We can spend the night discussing the

life and times of old saloon girls,
Waddya think Maria.'

Maria sniffed loudly. 'It'll take
more than one night to tell that tale
Martha.' She grinned and pointed to
the half empty bottle of whiskey.
'Best bring that drink with you
Martha, we have got plenty to
discuss.'

Printed in Poland
by Amazon Fulfillment
Poland Sp. z o.o., Wrocław

53897883R00076